W9-CAW-248

Miss Lina's Ballerinas

By Grace Maccarone

Illustrated by Christine Davenier

FEIWEL AND FRIENDS

New York

To Jean Feiwel—G. M.

Pour Alain Davesne, mon oncle et professeur de danse, qui n'a pas
eu le bonheur de découvrir en moi une future étoile, mais qui m'a fait
rêver lorsque j'avais six ans sur Coppelia et le Lac des Cygnes . . .
je m'en souviens si bien—C. D.

A FEIWEL AND FRIENDS BOOK
An Imprint of Macmillan

MISS LINA'S BALLERINAS. Text copyright © 2010 by Grace Maccarone.
Illustrations copyright © 2010 by Christine Davenier. All rights reserved.
Distributed in Canada by H.B. Fenn and Company, Ltd.
Printed in October 2010 in the United States of America by Lehigh Phoenix,
Rockaway, New Jersey. For information, address Feiwel and Friends,
175 Fifth Avenue, New York, N.Y. 10010.

Library of Congress Cataloging-in-Publication Data Available

ISBN: 978-0-312-38243-8

Book design by Elizabeth Tardiff

Feiwel and Friends logo designed by Filomena Tuosto

First Edition: 2010

10 9 8 7 6 5 4 3 2

www.feiwelandfriends.com

In a cozy white house, in the town of Messina,

eight little girls studied dance with Miss Lina.

Christina, Edwina, Sabrina, Justina,

Katrina, Bettina, Marina, and Nina.

In pink head to toe, they practiced all day—
plié, relevé, pirouette, and *jeté.*

They danced doing math.

They danced while they read.

And after their supper, they danced into bed.

They danced at the park.

They danced at the zoo.

They danced at the beach,
in four lines of two.

Christina, Edwina, Sabrina, Justina,

Katrina, Bettina, Marina, and Nina.

They danced at the market where they did their shopping.

In four lines of two, they danced without stopping.

Then one sunny morning, a girl named Regina
arrived at the cozy white house in Messina.

Miss Lina announced, in her elegant way,
"A new ballerina will join us today.
This is Regina. Her dancing is fine."
Miss Lina's eight dancers had turned into nine.

Then eight ballerinas cried, "What shall we do?
With nine, we no longer make four lines of two."

Christina, Edwina, Sabrina, Justina,
Katrina, Bettina, Marina, and Nina.

Annoyed and irate, distraught and distressed,
the girls started dancing, and oh, what a mess!

Christina bumped into Regina and Nina,
who stepped on Edwina, who fell on Sabrina.
Then down came Justina, and down came
Katrina, Bettina, Marina, and even Miss Lina!

The girls were abashed, baffled, befuddled,
flummoxed and flustered, mixed-up and muddled.

"There, there," said Miss Lina. "You will soon see how delightful it is to be three rows of three."

In three rows of three,
they practiced all day—
plié, relevé, pirouette, and *jeté.*

In three rows of three, they danced while they read.

They danced doing math

and going to bed.

At the park,

at the zoo,

at the beach,

and while shopping,

in three rows of three,
they danced without stopping.

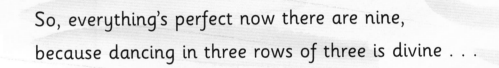

So, everything's perfect now there are nine,
because dancing in three rows of three is divine . . .

for Christina, Edwina, Sabrina, Justina,
Katrina, Bettina, Marina, and Nina

who dance all day long
with their new friend, Regina!

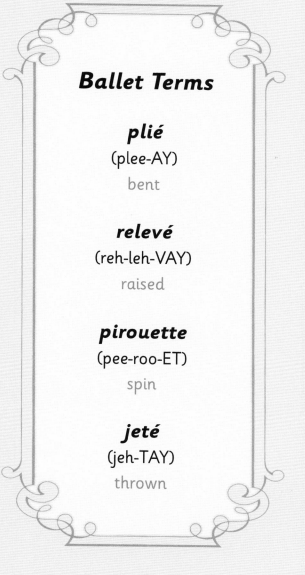

Ballet Terms

plié
(plee-AY)

bent

relevé
(reh-leh-VAY)

raised

pirouette
(pee-roo-ET)

spin

jeté
(jeh-TAY)

thrown